# Stand And Deliver

## HIGHWAYMAN STORIES AND SONGS

### RACHEL LAWSON

# Contents


Fullpage image 1

1. The King's Man 2

2. Shadows in the Daylight 25

3. All Or Nothing 31

4. The Ride of the Highwaymen 38

5. The Midnight Requiem 40

6. The Rise of the Ghost - A Novelette 44

Fullpage image 60

7. The Clown Show 61

8. Shadows in the Moonlight 69

9. In the Moonlight: a highwayman song 79

10. Midnight Requiem song 81

11. The Ghost of Your Gaze or The Ghost's Serenade a song 82

12. Dick Turpin & the King of the Road a Song 85

13.  Death Called To Me                                    87

About the author                                          89

Blurb                                                     91

# CHAPTER ONE

# The King's Man

On a cool crisp night in the Epping Forest, a stagecoach was moving amongst the shadows of a full silver moon.

"the moonlight gives the forest a magical glow", said Mary Gregory a

passenger in the coach. The other passenger was her brother, Magistrate Sir Thomas Gregory, but he thought it felt less magical but

more eerie and dangerous. He saw highwaymen and footpads in every

shadow. The driver was also very nervous as highwaymen were known to

work within these woods.

Suddenly a handsome well dressed man carrying a brace of gleaming duelling pistols  appeared, He was riding a white horse and had come out

of the shadows into the moonlight.

The nervous driver sped up the coach.

The horseman was following the coach but at a faster pace, shouting "Stop now or I'll shoot!"

"Stand and deliver, your money or your life!" shouted the highwayman
Firing his pistol he winged the driver who knowing the next shot might
kill him slowed the coach to a stop.

The rider caught up to them and stopping his horse he dismounted. Mary and her brother climbed out of the coach.

"Ah,  good evening my lady and Sir Thomas Gregory.  It is a lovely evening is it not?" said the Highwayman as he kissed Mary's hand.

"Oh yes, it is!" responded Mary enchanted by the moonlight and his gallantry.

"No, it is not, I would rather have missed this meeting Faulkner!" said the Magistrate recognising him from wanted posters.

"Faulkner? Not Gentleman John Faulkner?" asked Mary.

"Guilty," said the highwayman smiling behind his mask.

"Your goods please Sir Thomas,"  demanded Faulkner pointing a gun at the Magistrate. Mary offered up her jewellery.

"Oh No keep your things, my lady," said Faulkner giving her jewellery

back. Her brother reluctantly handed him his purse of money.

The highwayman next turned to the driver Whose arm was bleeding badly

and holding out his hand for more booty John said.  "Now you sir, you

should get that arm looked at it looks quite bad!" the driver handed

over his valuables.

The Highwayman sent them on their way with Sir Thomas driving, and

the driver inside the coach being tended to by his sister Mary.

Two nights later with the weather warmer, a new highwayman was on the road for the first time.

It seemed to be a youth in a black outfit who was enjoying the thrill of

riding through the night.  It was the first outing of this new highwayman.

This highwayman nearly held up a coach, but he was beaten to it by

another highwayman. He saw this from a hill where he was waiting for the

Coach to arrive. So he turned his horse and headed dejectedly home.

The next morning the Gregory home had a visitor.

Mary was very excited to meet a famous man she had never met before. He

was an actor who is famous for playing the part of the black highwayman

on stage.

He was a tall handsome man and from the moment Mary saw him she knew she

could easily love him, this man's name was Sir Justin Beaufort.

"Hello my lady," said the Actor, "I hear that you met a real highwayman

the other day I wish I had been with you. They are so thrilling and romantic!"

"Yes they are," agreed Mary.

"No, they are dangerous mercenaries! The driver of the coach died from

the wound he got from the highwayman or did you forget that,"
asked Sir

Thomas.

Sir Justin looked chastened and nervous.

"Did he have a family," asked Sir Justin.

"More than likely and they'll hang Faulkner now he's killed someone," said Sir Thomas.

"He won't hang! It was an accident," said Mary.

"He shot the man he should have realised there was a chance the
man would die!" said Sir Thomas.

"If they get him they will hang him, I'm sure of that!," said Sir Justin
sadly.

Later Mary was riding in a coach with Sir Justin and she heard.

"Stand and deliver your money or your life," The voice yelled.

When the coach stopped she leapt out of the coach to see the driver
being murdered with a single shot to the heart. For no other reason
than
that he didn't stop quickly enough.

She was now nervous. This was the feared killer highwayman Terrence the Terror of Essex.

"Hand over your loot! Either give it to me now or I will take it from your body!" Terrence the Terror said to her.

She climbed out quickly and out of the coach also stepped an angry Sir Justin.

"That's enough Terry.  Give it all back !" said Sir Justin.

This startled the Terror who was confused. Sir Justin walked over disarmed him and pointed the Terror's own gun at him.

"I said give it back Terry," said Sir Justin.

"Don't call him Terry people say he doesn't like that, This isn't the theatre he'll kill you," said Mary nervously.

"He'll have to wait in line," said Sir Justin with a smile.

"Sir Justin you are annoying me. Nobody robs me not even my friends you
will pay for this stand down and I will forget it," said Terrence the Terror.

"Stand and deliver Terry," said Sir Justin.

"He is drunk ignore him, Mister Terror," said Mary.

"He's stone-cold sober and stubborn," said the highwayman.

Terrence the Terror handed back the loot but he was fuming.

Sir Justin shot in the air to disarm the gun.

"Here you are my friend, have your property, and let us go on our way," said Sir Justin

"You are not my friend," said Terrence the Terror stomping over to his horse.

"You know something I think I have lost a friend," said Sir Justin sadly as he drove the coach off.

"You are insane," shouted back Mary from inside the coach.

Later in the day at the Gregory home.

"Tom your friend is a nut," Mary said when they arrived with the body of the driver.

"What did he do murder the driver so he could drive the coach?" asked Sir Thomas.

Sir Justin laughed.

"No that was Terrence the Terror," said Sir Justin.

"Oh did he kill the driver so you could drive it," said Sir Thomas

"Are you insane," asked Sir Justin.

"No," said Sir Thomas

"Terrence the Terror held us up, he shot the driver, then I held up the Terror," said Sir Justin.

"You did what, " asked Sir Thomas.

"I bailed up the Terror and took your sister's stuff back as she was under my care!" said Sir Justin.

"Thank you did you take him in," asked Sir Thomas.

"No! I let him go," said Sir Justin.

"Why did you do that!" asked Sir Thomas.

"Someone had to drive the coach, and I could not be sure of Mary's safety if I kept him," replied Sir Justin.

"You know that he'll now try to kill you!" said Sir Thomas.

"If he does he does!  I could never live with myself if he robbed someone under my care!" replied Sir Justin.

That night the youthful highwayman rode again.

This time he stopped a coach and started to rob people when three highwaymen arrived on the scene.

"New to this are you lad!" said one of them.

The youth panicked and fell off the horse banging his head hard and was knocked out by the fall.

"Terry I think you killed him!" said one of the others he was the black-clad highwayman  named the Ghost for his sudden appear-ances and

disappearances

"Ghost the boy's knocked out Not dead," said Gentleman John who was riding with them.

"Terry just scared him," said John.

"We can't leave him here what will we do!" said the Highwayman the Ghost,  a Robin Hood-type highwayman.

They completed the robbery.

John picked the body up and hung it over his horse.

The Ghost took the horse of the young highwayman and they rode off to Gentleman John's house.

"I'll look after him till he comes round," offered John.

The odd band of highwaymen sat drinking and chatting for a few hours and
then the Terror and the ghost left. When they had gone John made a
strange discovery the boy had long hair in a bun and his hat had been
pinned to it. He found this out when he tried to remove the hat so he
could put the lad to rest on his bed.

He put her on the bed and sat looking at a script for a new play.

He then sat drinking for a while.

Later when the highway woman woke up it was like a play with a ham actor.

"Where am I?" she muttered.

Putting down the script he walked over to her.

"How are you feeling Miss?" asked John.

"Miss?'" said the highwaywoman not sure how he knew what she was or where she was.

She felt for her mask it was there.

"I saw your hair! If we knew you were a woman my friends would have stayed," said John.

"Why?" she asked.

"For your honour," said John, "Whoever said there is no honour among thieves?"

"Oh yes," said the highwaywoman

"Nothing happened but I'll marry you to keep your honour," said John.

The highwaywoman stood up still a bit wonky. She thought she was dreaming he was a man of honour and she loved him so she was happy.

She started to take off her mask and he stopped her.

"No don't," said John. "we aren't safe, Seeing each other's faces may cause us problems!"

"All right then," She said and stopped trying to unmask.

In the early morning, she said goodbye and left for home.

A few hours later, Mary was sitting in the forest near her home enjoying the new autumn day.

Sir Justin saw her on the way to visit her brother.

He got off his horse and tied it to a branch of a small tree and walked over to her.

"What are you doing my lady?" asked Sir Justin thinking she looked very pretty sitting amongst the autumn leaves.  She blushed.

"It is ethereal here today!" said  Mary looking at Sir Justin who looked more handsome than ever.

"It is a glorious day!" said Sir Justin not lying,

"Are you alright?"

"Yes, come sit beside me," said Mary.

"Why?" asked Sir Justin.

"The view is best from here," said Mary.

"As long as no one's around!" said Sir Justin.

With a smile, she said, "No one is here!"

Sir Justin sat beside her.

"What are we looking at?" asked Sir Justin.

"Everything the wind is singing in the trees blowing leaves through the

air as they fall to the ground. The birds are singing and the forest floor is covered in crisp leaves thick as snow," said Mary.

Forgetting propriety and everything. He lay on his back in the leaves.

"I have never seen anything so beautiful, I could forget everything and

live here in this moment forever." then looking up at the sky He said,

"This looks better!"

Mary lay back too she watched the leaves fall from the trees blowing in

the wind. A leaf fell down floating onto her heart she put her hand on

it.

A voice interrupted the scene.

"Ah there you are, Mary, have you been with him all night? Every-one has been looking for you!" accused Sir Thomas.

"No!" Sir Justin said standing. "I just found her here, I was on my way to see you."

Mary trying to stand up fell over her long skirt.

"I was not with him," said Mary.

Sir Justin thought he could see a forced Marriage wedding being set up.

"I can't marry her," said Sir Justin.

"Why?" asked Sir Thomas.

"I can't say, " said Sir Justin.

"No excuses means that you must marry her for your honour and hers," said Sir Thomas.

"Don't use my honour against me," said Sir Justin.

"You must Marry her as you are driven by your honour," Sir Thomas said.

Sir Justin shook his head jumped on his horse and rode away.

Later that day Sir Justin sat with his friend the Earl of Essex  the cousin of Gentleman Jack in their friend the King's library chatting.

"How was your day Sir Justin," asked the king.

"Great I became Engaged," said Sir Justin.

"Congratulations," replied the Earl with a strong French accent.

"Who is she? asked the king.

"The sister of a friend of mine," said Sir Justin.

"Who is your friend," asked the Earl.

"A Magistrate from  Loughton," said Sir Justin.

"Not your friend Sir Thomas Gregory," asked the Earl.

"Yes, his sister," said Sir Justin taking a sip of wine.

"His sister is lovely she'll make a good wife for you," the Earl said.

"She thinks I'm a madman," Sir Justin said taking another sip.

"Why on Earth would she think that?" asked the King.

"I bailed up the Terror,"  said Sir Justin drawing a big sip of wine.

"You did what?" asked the Earl excitedly.

"Why on Earth would you do that?" asked the King.

"She was under my care and the Terror held us up I was protecting her," said Sir Justin.

"So you robbed him," said the Earl.

"You are lucky to be alive the Terror is a killer," said the King.

"I know, he killed the driver," said Sir Justin.

"He'll try to kill you for that," said the King.

"He'll be doing me a service," said Sir Justin.

"Are you alright?" asked the Earl.

"I don't want to marry that girl," Sir Justin said.


Later Sir Justin went to the Earl's blacksmith David Buckingham's shop to get his horse re-shod.

"Master Buckingham how are things going with your business to-day," asked Sir Justin.

"Good  I have been very busy today," said David as he re-shod the horse.

"Your horse is very calm today,'" said David.

"Yes I fed her before we came, it calms her down," said Sir Justin.

A soldier walked into the smithy.

"Where is my gun!" demanded the soldier.

"I am busy please come back later, sir," said David.

"No, I want it now!" snapped the soldier impatiently.

"Patience is a virtue," said the smith.

"I have not time for words," said the soldier kicking the smith which startled the horse which then kicked the smith in the guts.

"My gun now, man!" said the impatient soldier not caring that the man was hurt.

"Stand away man!" said Sir Justin pulling out his gun, "are you alright?"

"I feel like I was kicked by a horse, Jack," said the Ghost.

The soldier looked puzzled.

Gentleman Jack Glared at the soldier.

The Ghost got the man's gun and gave it to him.

"I fixed it now pay the fee we agreed to and be on your way," the Ghost said.

The soldier paid him and left.

"We need to get you to the doctor," said Jack helping his friend onto

David's horse and jumped on too and rode David the Ghost to his doctor.

Later Jack dropped the Ghost off in town he did what any man who'd been
kick by a horse would do he went to the pub and drank a little too much.

When he was drinking he heard a soldier talking about his old friend from the wars who was still a soldier being set before a firing squad for the crime of another soldier.

"Do you want a blindfold?" asked the Captain of the regiment.

"No!" Malcolm Giles the man being shot called back.

"Ready! Aim! Fie," was all the captain called he saw 3 highwaymen aiming at him.

"Shoot and your Captain's dead," shouted Jack.

"Faulkner stand tell your friends to stand down this man is to get his
justice" shouted Captain Terrence Norton aka the Terror.

"No he was framed," the Ghost shouted back.

"No he was not," shouted Terry.

"Release him," ordered Jack.

"Do as he says," barked Terry not wanting to be shot.

"Silver Buckles take the man his horse," said the Ghost to the highway

woman she did as she was told they had brought a spare horse for
Malcolm.

He leaped onto it and they rode off in a hail of bullets.


"Sir Thomas a soldier is here to see you," said the housekeeper of the
Gregory house to her master.

"Show him into the library I'll talk to him there," said Sir Thomas.

A little time later in the Gregory library, the Soldier was shown in.

It was Captain Terrence Norton.

"What is your name Captain?" asked Sir Thomas.

"I would rather not say, I am here to help you catch a highwayman,"
Terry said.

"Why?" asked Sir Thomas.

"I would rather not say," Terry said.

"I hear you want to catch the highwayman, John Faulkner," said Terry.

"Yes," said Sir Thomas.

Over the following weeks, the Highwayman and Highwaywoman became

inseparable and took to the road most nights. They planned to run away

and marry after one last job but it all went wrong.  There was an unexpected ambush.

They were on their horses and when they demanded the passengers disembark the coach. They didn't notice the gun pointing from the coach

until it was too late. But when they did they rode away it was Sir Thomas who shot one of them.

John could have escaped. But he jumped off his running horse which

continued on its way. He ran back to his fiancée the Highway woman

"You shot her," said John accusingly.

Kneeling down cradling her and looking into her face.

"Why didn't you escape," asked the dying Highway woman.

"I don't want to live without you," said John.

"I have the two of them, I shall unmask them," said Sir Thomas. unmasking John his eyes widened and looked horrified.

"Hi!" said Sir Justin.

"But, You are engaged to my sister! Who is this Harlot," asked Sir Thomas ripping off her mask. Looking devastated.

"Mary, No." cried Sir Thomas.

"Mary my other fiancée," said John.

"My love," said Mary and died.

John kissed her for the first and last time.


"The Earl of Essex and someone called Captain Norton from Loughton are
here to see John Faulkner," said the guard to the prison administrator.

"Essex, he's his cousin, OK, Let him go in," said the administrator.

They were taken to Jack's cell and left alone to talk to him.

"Jack, I'm sorry about what happened I didn't want anyone to die," said Terry.

"We're here to break you out," said the Earl.

"You can't you'd be revealing yourselves as the Terror and the Ghost, Drew," said Jack.

"We don't care anymore," said Terry.

"We only want to see you free," said the Earl, who was the Ghost.

"I don't want to live without Mary," said Jack, "thanks but I just want to be with Mary in the hereafter."

"Goodbye Jack we will miss you," said the Ghost.

"I'll miss you holding me up," joked the Terror, "Goodbye," he said "she

was worth holding up a friend over and I hope you and she will find happiness in your next life."

"I'll see your body is buried near your Mary," said the Earl hugging his cousin one last time.

"Thank you," said Jack,"goodbye until we meet again in the here-after."

With that, the Ghost and the Terror left Jack to his fate in his cell.

A few weeks later John joined her in death.

As John was standing on the gallows at Tyburn.

Sir Thomas watched the noose go around John's neck  Sir Thomas
was sad he
knew he'd miss John and Sir Justin.  The executioner reached for
and
pulled the lever for the trap door. Then the Magistrate closed his
eyes.
He saw Mary and John lying in the leaves in the forest and he heard
John
saying "I have never seen anything so beautiful! I could forget
everything and live in this moment forever"

# CHAPTER TWO

# Shadows in the Daylight

The highwayman sat atop his great warhorse with an air of confidence and absolute charm as he told the passengers to alight from their coach to Loughton from London. He was strong and handsome and utterly madly fashionable actually he set the trends of fashion in London all women loved him and the men were either jealous of his fascinating all the women there or else wanted to be him. Most of them dressed like him but totally hated him.

So was the case with Isabella Constance and the man who virtually worshipped her, but she was in love with the romantic highwayman, the Viscount of Essex John Faulkner the perfect gallant gentleman he was the most charming handsome, and romantic  highwayman beside his constant companion on the road a clever escape artist who disappeared into the shadows of the dark of night on the lonely forest road to New Market,

The companion was as well-built and handsome as the Viscount and his tale was that a penitent and even a more romantic highwayman He was a lovelorn, brokenhearted man who went to war with the local garrison instead of staying to protect his fiancée who died when he fought to put the king on the throne of his executed father, and although he took a bullet which saved the king's life

he returned to find his lady and her family had died poor of starvation. The man took to the road to see her fate never befell anyone else. He was a Robin Hood who robbed only those who could afford to lose a little money which he gave to an obliging churchman called Prideaux who promised he would give it to the poor in his parish.

"Lieutenant Faulkner and the Ghost too, this is my lucky day!" Isabella sang in her joy to the man who loved her, but she couldn't love, let alone see

"I can't see why we should be happy to be robbed!" Stephen Grimshaw said irritably in reply.

He was angry and wanted to protect her and his money and a poem he wrote secretly to her anonymously as he had many times before. She knew she had a secret admirer but not his name, he was called Silver Starr and a poet in love with her.

"What light from yonder window breaks it is Juliet!" said Faulkner seeing her charmingly.

"Ham is not your style, Jack," said the Ghost scolded.

"Right, you are, Drew! Pray, excuse me my dear lady I was dazzled by your eyes they are like 2 twinkling silver stars! Was I out of line?" Jack said contritely.

"Here is my money and ring everyone gives me your money and stuff, and they'll let us go!" said Grimshaw sharply as he glared at Jack.

"Yes! Said the Ghost.

"Oh yes!" said Jack.

They gave the awkward highwayman what they wanted, and they forgot to speak.

"Bye then," said Grimshaw.

"You can go Adieu!" The Ghost said with a strangely French accent and not his usual

local Essex accent he was noted for. When the coach was gone the highwaymen tore off their own masks.

"Justin, what was that about? What light on yonder window breaks-! Your eyes are like 2 twinkling silver stars!" shouted the Ghost.

"She's a friend of mine! You know she hates me as much as I hate her! If I said Isabella give me  your money I would be giving myself away and what about you the French Ghost"

"I forgot who I was I knew the man with her, he's my friend Stephen Grimshaw. He's a minor poet, and he's in love with the girl. He's been sending her love letter from what I've found out from being his go-between he uses the nom de plume of Silver Starr. She's fallen in love with her admirer now if I'm not mistaken she thinks you are him! This won't make Grimshaw happy at all!" the Ghost said.

"He's not happy! How do you think I am I'm engaged to two women already  why not go for the trifecta and have more people wanting to see me dancing on the stage at Tyburn!" Jack said turning his horse to face his cousin the Earl of Essex,

"Robert what do you want me to do we have made her hate me and love your friend he wants her I don't!" Jack said.

"Easy he's coming to my home she is too! They'll be at my party!" said the Earl.

"Oh we can use that!" said Jack.

"How Justin?" asked the Earl.

"By making her hate me and love him!" said Jack.

"Tell her who you are!" joked the Ghost,

"Very funny it won't work," Jack said, "She'd lynch me herself!"

"Fine, I'll supply the tree! The old oak out the front of my place would be perfect, and I'll buy her a nice strong rope!" Joked the Ghost.

"Who are you 2 planning to hang?" A soldier who they didn't see arrive, "Can I help you?"

"Hello, Terry! We don't want anyone dead! I was only joking! Let's go Home!" The Earl said to his friends who lived at his house as his live-in guests with the run of the house.

They were the earl's maternal cousin and the youngest son of another earl whose wife and twin brother died when he was born and was taken in by Jack who, although she had the blood of the earl of Essex and was the aunt of the present orphaned earl of Essex and was his guardian

She raised him when he was in hiding as Andrew Fletcher, a blacksmith's apprentice. His master's daughter was the Earl's fiancée.

"Your Ladyship is well I hope?" said lord Essex when Isabella and Grimshaw entered his sitting room, his library of books and oddments with many maps, old weapons, and comfy chairs and a well-used desk well made of metalwork of the earl himself as a secret but famed blacksmith as David Buckingham.

"We were held up by highwaymen!" said Grimshaw.

"Was anything stolen?" asked Jack with an air of concern, mocking the cause he knew he'd stolen the poor girl's heart.

"Yes, they were highwaymen, I said they robbed us! Didn't I in a roundabout way!" Grimshaw said.

"He's thick as well as heartless he's the most annoying actor on any stage in London, ignore him he's a bore!" said Isabella.

"Do you have a name, sir?" asked Grimshaw.

"I'm an actor, I've had many!" Said Jack.

"Jack!" the earl snapped, "when you are good and when you are bad, you're horrid!"

"Jack! Are you a highwayman?" asked Grimshaw, sure he was talking to his rival the viscount but why would the earl of Essex be a highwayman

"Only at certain times!" said Jack, "not permanently!"

"What are you on John Faulkner, the viscount of Essex!" Grimshaw said

"Pardon me? Oh yes, yes, and he's the Ghost!" Jack said.

"What, you admit it? Why did his lordship take to the road!" said Grimshaw.

"Take to the road? Oh? I didn't take to the road, neither did he! We leave that to my real cousin Jack! This man is Sir Justin Beaufort, he and I took to the London stage in the theatre in about Jack and his friends, I play the Ghost in it. Sir Justin plays Jack, so I call him Jack nothing more I use a stage name to keep it quiet." said the Earl, "there is nothing sinister there!"

"Only that horse of mine in it is the only strange thing, and the script isn't either well written either!" said Jack.

"Thanks, Jack, you know you have the playwright in here!" said Terry.

"I know I want a real horse and script even I could ad-lib better lines so could all the cast, why is the Ghost the only one without a script!" Jack complained.

"I memorized them before I rehearsed the play!" the Earl said, "and I only ad-lib in emergencies, know that Jack!"

"There's always an emergency!" protested Jack, "You usually cause it!"

"Don't fight we have guests," Terry said afraid one of them would say something they all might regret like the 3 of them were real highwaymen

and then he'd have to kill these people who held them as friends.

Terry hated being the bad guy who everyone saw as purely evil or insane he was just as twitchy as the Ghost was, but the Ghost wasn't ill, and the Ghost wasn't short-tempered nor did he feel he was the one who had to do the killing if it had to be done as it was expected Terry not them.

Terry could only hang once and if he and Jack too as he winged a man who died of his wounds. The Ghost may not hang, he may be deported or spend some time in prison, he hadn't done anything more than highway robbery.

# CHAPTER THREE

# All Or Nothing

"Who is this young man, he has the air of a lord," said Lord Hawthorne a

gentleman from a small Yorkshire town in his ballroom he was having a

country dance. "He is Andrew Fletcher, he's newly rich he's from

London," said Sir Kenneth Stanton, Lord Hawthorne's oldest friend who

knew everything going on in town. "He seems to like my daughter a lot,"

said Lord Hawthorne, "I think I should speak to him, she is wide-eyed and naive, I don't want him breaking her heart." "Yes," said Sir Kenneth.

They walked over to his pretty daughter Amy and her suitor. "Hello, Amy," said the Lord to his daughter. "Hello, Papa," said Amy. "Who is your new friend?" asked Lord Hawthorne of Andrew, who looked nervous.

"He's Andrew Fletcher, he's newly from London," said Amy. "Hello, sir," said Andrew. "That's an Essex accent, not a London one," said Lord Hawthorne, suspecting he was lying about himself. "I am originally from Loughton in Essex," said Andrew, trying to cover up and make an excuse for his accent, he was in fact from Loughton, Essex. "You meet many highwaymen there?" asked the lord trying to test his honesty, he'd been there, and it was a hotbed of highwaymen. "A few! They are hard to avoid there," said Andrew, not lying. "The Ghost, and the Terror of

Essex, are from Loughton too," said Lord Hawthorne. "Yes," said Andrew,

trying to hide his nerves as he planned to escape if he needed to. He

was in fact one of the highwaymen, who mentioned he feared he was

caught. He

knew the lord from his work on the road, he'd held him up. "Stop

grilling him, you are scaring him," said Amy. "Sorry, man," said the

lord. "Thank you, Miss Amy, they scare me," said the ghost, smiling

charmingly. "Yes, they are brutes," said Amy. The Ghost felt guilty for

what he was doing to the girl, he had to seduce her to get close to her

father which so far wasn't working on her father she seemed an inno-

cent

girl who he would have wanted to protect from rogues like himself

usually, but he had a method behind his treachery. He was desperate

to

save a life. He felt he had no other option than to be a cold-hearted

cad. It was all or nothing to him, so The Ghost, who was in truth a lord he was the Earl of Essex, and had no other choice but to go against his

principles. "Drew," another man behind him said. "Yes," Andrew said, he

was happy to be reminded he wasn't alone in his quest to save a friend.

The Terror sensing his nerves put his hand on his back to comfort his

young friend. Andrew smiled. "Go dance with her," said Terry the terror.

Amy smiled at Andrew. "Yes," said the father. Amy and Andrew walked

away and danced. Terry watched them, Andrew was an expert but nervous

dancer. Terry thought they looked a perfect match. He felt sad to think

Andrew was not at all interested in the girl. He was too good an actor.

She was only a means to a greater end. Andrew rode with her every day

and became close to her and her family, as was the plan. "Mr Fletcher

what are your intentions with my Daughter," one-day lord Hawthorne asked

Andrew, seeing their relationship was getting serious. Andrew stood

dumbstruck for a moment, not sure what to say. He wanted to run away,

but for the first time in his life, he couldn't move. He thought all he

could do was ask for her hand, her father accepted his plea if his

daughter accepted him too. She accepted his hand in marriage. Later that

day, Andrew sat drunk and tried to become more plastered in the pub.

Sadly, hours after, the even more plastered Highwayman held up the

Hawthornes. He was unmasked and recognised as Andrew. The next day, a

sober Andrew went to see Amy, he complained about blacking out and

forgetting where he was the previous night. They looked at him, knowing who

he was. Hawthorne called in some soldiers who were there to talk to the

victims about the robbery. Andrew didn't know what was happening. He'd forgotten the robbery. Amy cried, accusing him of robbing them last

night. He thought his plan had failed, and he wasted his time and felt

worse for what he did to the girl. He was in shock. He tried to run but

was captured. The devastated man was put in prison waiting for his

trial. There he met a friend in his cell. They were taken from their

cell by a soldier, who took them from the prison to see a judge, or so

the soldier said. He actually took them to horses. "Thank you for
saving

me, my friends," the man Andrew met in prison said. "You're welcome,

Jack," said Andrew. "How did you get in prison and get me out."
Andrew's

Cousin the highwayman, Jack Faulkner, asked. "Don't ask!" said the

soldier Captain Norton, the Terror. Andrew looked ashamed. They
rode off

home, never to return to the area again, as they were revealed as highwaymen.

# CHAPTER FOUR

# The Ride of the Highwaymen

The air bore the chilling nip of winter, and the highwayman's horse skipped across the snowy road to New Market from London.

His and his companion's breath formed clouds as they breathed.

The lightly falling snow looked like magic as they rode down the road at full pace after a mark. Their mark was a lone rider who had strayed on the stomping ground, it seemed.

The rider sped up, hoping in vain that he would lose his pursuers, who were quickly catching up to him,

"Stand and deliver!" cried one of the highwaymen, aiming a gun at the rider.

The rider stopped.

"Ok, Jack, you win," said the rider to the highwayman Gentleman Jack.

"Terry, Ghost it's my turn to play the mark," said Jack to the rider and his companion

"Fine with me," the rider who was their bored friend Terence, the Terror of Essex another highwayman.

"Me too," said the equally bored highwayman, the Ghost.

It was a quiet night they hadn't seen anyone to rob all night so they resorted to hunting each other.

# CHAPTER FIVE

# The Midnight Requiem

"S tand and Deliver, Your money or your-" said a highwayman pulling over a

rich-looking man who looked impatient. "I know that!" said the mark

impatiently, he hadn't the time to be robbed by an amateur he was late

for a visit with the king. "I have a gun," said the highwayman. "I can

see that I'm not blind," said the fat pigeon. "Give me your bag, my fat

pigeon," said the bandit. "Not that, go high jack a real pigeon, I'm late

for an appointment," shouted the rich man who tried to disarm the

highwayman, but he was knocked out and robbed. "This is what the bandit

had on him when we caught him, Sir," said a soldier to the king's

Thief-Taker, Sir Thomas Gregory. Sir Thomas took the bag and looked at

the contents, he found an item that caught his attention. It was a music

manuscript, he walked over to a piano and started to perform the song.

"Darkness conceals its beauty within an aura of fear,

Night to me is something dear,

In the coolness of the night, I ride,

The wary do cautiously hide,

In fear of me and my cast,

I alone see the night's beauty to its hour's last,

Like a thief in the night,

When I'm seen, I disappear like a ghost out of sight," he sang. Then stopped singing. "What do you think about it?" asked the Thief-Taker.

"It was good," said the soldier. "Anything else?" asked Sir Thomas.

"What else is there?" asked the soldier. "It was sung by the highway-man

the Ghost last week when he pulled over Lord Harry Scott," said Sir Thomas. "So?" said the soldier, not sure where the Thief Taker was going. "This looks to be the original manuscript of the song," said Sir

Thomas. "Alright," said the soldier. "I think they held up the Ghost and

stole his sheet music," said Sir Thomas. "Why would he do that?" asked

the soldier. "I think it was an accident, it must have been in the bag," said, Sir Thomas. "You think the bag belonged to the Ghost?" said the

soldier. "Yes," said Sir Thomas. "I don't see anything that identifies him," said the soldier. "The manuscript has his name on it," said Sir Thomas. The soldier looked at it and looked puzzled. "Where?" asked the

soldier. "It is in his hand," said Sir Thomas. "What's the chance of us

identifying the owner?" asked the soldier. In the room walked a man.

"Hello, my lord," said Sir Thomas. "Have you seen Sir Justin?" asked the

man. "He's late," said the Thief-Taker. "Who is his lordship?" asked the soldier curiously. "The Earl of Essex," said Sir Thomas. The Earl spied on the music. "You got some new music oh nice mind if I try it, while

I wait for him," the Earl said with his French accent. "Alright, my Lord," said Sir Thomas. He sat and sang the song as he played the music.

"Nice music, mind if I borrow it," the Earl asked offhandedly. "No we

are trying to study it?" said the Thief-Taker. "Oh really? Who wrote it?

I want a copy," asked the Earl. "We think it was the highwayman, the

Ghost," said Sir Thomas. "He's good," said the Earl. The soldier wasn't

enjoying hearing the song sung by the Earl, who had a strong French

accent.


"Shut up, My lord, you are killing my ears," said Sir Justin walking into

the room. "Philistine!" hissed the Earl standing up to greet his friend.

"Phillis, don't call me a lady," joked Sir Justin. "He's a fool," said a

lady who entered the room with Sir Justin. Sir Justin glared at the

lady. "Hello Mary," said Sir Thomas to his sister. The Earl felt sorry

for his friend, the lady was his friend's fiancé and they hated each

other. The Earl picked up the music and looked at it distracted, he fell

over dropping it into the blazing fire in the chimney. "No," screamed

Sir Thomas, runs to the fire, trying to salvage the destroyed sheet

music. "You fool, you destroyed the evidence that would have given us

the Ghost on a platter," shouted the angry, Thief-Taker. "I'm sorry, Sir

Thomas," said the Earl contritely as he stood up. Sir Justin shot the

Earl had an amused look. He knew something Sir Thomas didn't

the Earl, was

the Ghost, and he had obviously planned to burn the evidence. Sir Thomas

was so mad with the Earl, he didn't speak to him for a week.

# CHAPTER SIX

# The Rise of the Ghost – A Novelette

S omewhere in England, on the old estate of a long-dead and nearly forgotten Earl of Essex. During a temporary amateur archaeological dig.

"We found something in trench 2, Dr Alexander it's what we expected,"

amateur archaeologist Ken Harley said to the head archaeologist Dr Stella Alexander. They dashed to the trench. "Where is the artefact?"

asked Stella excitedly. "Over there, Charlie's cleaning it," said another archaeologist who was still digging in the trench.

"Ok," said Stella, then she and Ken went to the tent which they used as a

lab it was a hot summer's day, so Stella enjoyed getting out of the
sun. It took a moment for her eyes to adjust to the light changing
to
the darkness of the tent. She saw Charlie standing in the corner of
the
tent, evidently cleaning something. She walked over to Charlie. Ken
followed her. "Hi Dr Alexander, Ken," said Charlie. "How is it?"
asked
Stella. "Better than I expected?" said Charlie, showing them the
artefact. It was a matte black modified duelling pistol, it was caked
in
dirt. "It looks amazing," said Stella. "How did you know where it
was?"
asked Ken. "Metal detector," lied Stella. "How did you know we
were
looking for a gun, anyway," said Ken. "I read about the Ghost's gun
being buried near here by his family," lied Stella. "It is really
well-made," said Ken. "The Ghost was the best blacksmith in Essex
in his
time," Stella said she knew everything about the Ghost she'd written a
book about him and practically worshipped him. "Here, hold it,"
said
Charlie, who knew she was a fan of the Ghost. Stella took the gun
in her
hands and felt something strange happen she couldn't explain. It
was
like a spark, and she saw what she could only think was a vision of
the
Renascence highwayman, the Ghost.

Meanwhile, on the other side of the world, a man another magician awoke

from a spell and was consumed by the soul of the Ghost. His sleeping

soul had awoke.


A moment later, a swirling wormhole appeared in the tent Stella walked

into it, leaving her confused spooked colleagues behind never to see

them again. On the other side of the wormhole, she met a man. "Thanks,

Uncle Temp," she said, hugging the man her great-great Uncle. "Your

welcome, Stella," said her Uncle Tempus, the Timekeeper. "I really

wanted to get this before it was stolen and destroyed by activists, it

is a treasure," said Stella. "Yes," said Tempus. "I saw him when I first

touched his gun," said Stella. "You did," said Tempus as if he knew

something he didn't want to tell her. "What is it?" she asked.

"Nothing," said Tempus lying. "It's time you returned to your own time

now," said Tempus. Ok but hide it close, guns are illegal in your time,

and the police will destroy it if they find it." said Tempus. "I will," said

Stella. "Take the portal over there to get home," said Tempus point-ing

at a vortex. She took it and appeared in the street 26 years after the

excavation in Melbourne, Australia, near her home. She hid the gun under her trench coat and walked home.

Later that week, Stella went to a masked ball for a forum run by her
father Prince Jasper's best friend as a member of the imperial family
of
the universe. The Celestial Emperor Sapphirus hugged her when he
saw
her, he was her a few times great-great-grandfather. "Hello
Gramps," she
said to him, "how is the ball going?" asked Stella"Good but, Aureus
is
late, he should be here for this as the local system's emperor,  your
dad's been covering for him, I wonder where he is?" said Sapphirus.
In
walked a man dressed as the Ghost. Stella looked awkwardly at him.
"Excuse me Gramps, I have to talk to someone," said Stella. "Ok,
have a
good night, Stella," said the celestial emperor. She walked over to
the
Ghost. "What are you doing?" said Stella. "I'm coming to the
masked ball
in style," said the Ghost. "In style, what are you going to do rob it?"
said, Stella. "Rob it?" said the Ghost, offended. "Why are you
dressed
as the Ghost?" asked Stella. "I was hoping to see Rogue Star," said
the
Ghost. Rogue Star was Stella's secret name as a local superhero. No
one
knew who she was. "Why?" asked Stella, frowning. "Do I need a
reason?"

said the Ghost. "Nice outfit, Aureus," said a voice behind them. "Hi, am

I that obvious?" said the Ghost. "Actually, yes," said Stella. "Well, I had to try, I wanted to meet Rogue Star," said Aureus. "Face it, she's out of your league," said the person behind them, Jasper her father. "I

am not the Masked Chicken now," said Aureus. Who had been a fool for

most of his life. He had been known as a fool, he had been known as the

Masked Chicken. He had indeed changed the man who woke up to be Aureus,

the Ghost. His sleeping soul awakening turned the hopeless, helpless,

fool into a normal person, but his reputation stuck. "We know it," said

Stella, "But you are no Ghost he is charming and amazing you are just...

you." Aureus looked sad that even the girl who loved the Ghost wasn't

mildly impressed by the outfit. "Well, I could be him, he is very

mysterious," said Aureus. "He's dead you aren't a ghost you can't be

dead, remember the last emperor of the solar system lost his job because

he was dead," said Stella. Jasper looked strangely at Sapphirus

awkwardly for some unknown reason known only to him and Sapphirus who

grimaced. "He wasn't dead, he was just the King of the Grim Reapers,"

said Aureus. "I wonder what happened to him?" said Stella. "I don't know, search me?" said Sapphirus. Up to them walked to the walked

Stella's Grandfather Lakelandite, the new king of the grim reapers. "Are

you hiding someone, Gramps," said Lakelandite said his grandfa-ther.

"No, go kill somebody you psychopath," grumbled back Sapphirus.

"Gramps!" Moaned Lakelandite.


Later on the police crime scene, Stella was hovering around in the

masked costume of Rogue Star with her father in his guise as the

Necromantor, the King of Doom. As they did, often as assistants of the

police. On the scene wandered the superhero the Ghost. Rogue's heart

raced, but she kept in control he had come to help too, it seemed. He

was evidently a magician himself as he was like them ageless and forever

young and solid. "Hi Ghost," said the Necromantor, "Good to see

you." "You too, Doom," said the Ghost. "Hello," was all Rogue could

force herself to say, she found it hard speaking around the Ghost.

"Hello, fair lady," said the Ghost, who had no problem with speak-ing,

Rogue felt funny about feeling like she did around the Ghost. She

wondered who he was and whether she knew him. A policeman walked up to

them. "Thanks for coming," he said to them, he was a magician too, He

was the Red Fox, "it is always good having a little help from my friends, come with me the coroner wants to see us." They walked over to

the body of a dead man. The coroner was examining a bullet hole in his

chest. "Hello, Dante," said the Ghost. "Hi Ghost, Doom, Rogue, what do

you think of the scene?" asked Dr Dante Drac with a voice that sounded

older than his body. He was another one of them too, a magician. "It's

good," said Rogue not sure what to say. "The man was shot from over

there," said Dante. "How do we know?" asked the Fox. "I was on the

scene," said Dante in a matter-of-fact tone. "Why didn't you save him?"

asked Rogue. "I was busy," said Dante. "Busy," said the Fox, puzzled. "I

had to take the soul in for processing," Dante said. "He's a reaper,"

said Doom, who'd seen him many times in the afterlife realm. "Oh ok, can

you ID the killer," said the Fox. "Yes," said Dante. "Seems like we

weren't needed here after all," the Ghost said. Rogue didn't see it that

way, she got to meet the Ghost again, so it wasn't a waste of time. The

Ghost waved, bade them goodbye and left again. Rogue felt dead inside,

she missed him. She teleported home to be greeted by her house-mate, her

cat. "I wonder where he goes, Tom," said Stella to the cat as she unmasked.

Elsewhere Aureus awoke from a black-out in a street, flustered and
confused where he had been and what he had been doing for the
last hour.

He rushed home to his housemate, scared and confused. When he
got

there he spoke to his housemate, he was a goldfish called Phineas
Fish.

"This is getting serious Phin these black-outs are getting worse,"
Aureus said to the fish who happily swam on oblivious to Aureus's
plight.

Later that week, Aureus met Stella again on a crime scene, this time
as

Aureus's alter ego the Rose. Aureus was obviously in love with
Rogue.

She knew him as her father's best friend so she wasn't interested in
him

and as they say familiarity breeds contempt it did with Stella, she

could not see him as anything but a friend and a bit of a stalker of
her

as Rogue Star. Truth was, she only had eyes for the Ghost. With
them was

the King of Doom and the King of the Earth (Sappirus in disguise)
this

time Sapphirus was looking at the body acting as coroner's assistant
to

Dante who was surprised how right Sapphirus was about the diag-
nosis of

the death of the victim. "Rogue," said Aureus. "Yes," said Stella

nervously, not wanting to encourage her suitor. "Why do you hide your

true identity from us," asked Aureus, "you know you can trust us with

your secret." "I am afraid if I do come out to the public I will have

problems as I am neither human nor totally Magician I am part X-Zeracien

people would treat me like a monster if they knew me," said Rogue who

lolookedok like a human with grey skin. "That's nothing to be ashamed of, I

was an idiot who thought he was a hero everyone had to save me," said

the Rose ashamed. "Your heart was in the right place," said Rogue

smiling behind her mask, trying to make him feel better. "How do you

know so much about the cause of death of the victim?" Dante asked

Sapphirus. "I'm over 200 you learn a few things over the years," said

Sapphirus who like all adult magicians only looked 25. Dante was

suspicious, but he let it ride. "You're kidding us you don't look that

old," said a policeman near them who was watching them diagnose the

victim. "My people can live forever we can only die if we are hurt, my

grandson Blake, you remember him Dr Alexander the coroner, he was over

1000 before he disappeared," said Sapphirus. "You mean the guy who disappeared because he was accused of murder," said the policeman. "He

was cleared," said Sapphirus. "Then why didn't he come back," asked the

policeman. "He said he moved on," said Doom who loved his granddad he

added, "People are allowed to move on aren't they?" "Yeah, I suppose," the

policeman said. Sapphirus smiled. "You know you can use an appearance

charm spell to make you look human all the Magicians do it will make you

look more human," said Aureus. "I may try that," said Rogue who used

the spell to change her hair from silver grey to black and her skin to a

more human tone like Stella's. "I have a friend who is a half-grey X-Zeracien alien, half Magician she uses the charm she looks very human," said Aureus. Doom smiled as if he knew something he wasn't

telling. He in fact knew his daughter's secret but he didn't know who

the Ghost was or he would have said something. He was not against his

daughter and the Ghost or even the Rose Aureus or anyone she liked being

together with her. He knew she was not interested in his friend so he

knew Aureus's was a lost case. "She's in love with somebody else," said

Jasper knowing Aureus was in love with Rogue a blind leper could tell

the Rose loved her but thought nothing of Stella. Her interest in the

Ghost was all-consuming. She saw Aureus as an admirer nothing serious.

"Who is it?" Aureus demanded. "You mean you don't know?" said a police

man nearby. " No? Who is he?" asked Aureus. "The Ghost," said Jasper,

"I'm so sorry my friend." "What? he's dead," said Aureus. Aureus bursting into tears stomped off.

When Stella got home she found a tear-stained Aureus sitting on her door

step and her neighbour mowing their lawn to keep an eye on the suspicious guest, they walked up to Stella and said the masked man had

been there for a while and they had called the police.

"Thank you, Terry, " said Stella. "You're welcome stay away from him he

looks dangerous," said Terry. "It's alright he's a friend," said Stella. Terry wondered what sort of a person befriended masked men. "Ok," said

Terry who continued mowing as he wondered who and what his neighbour

was. Stella wandered over to the masked man. "Hi Aureus are you alright? Come inside, I'll get you a drink," Stella told him helping him

up. "Thank you," said Aureus. She unlocked the door and let him in
feeling guilty for his misery. "Rogue Star," said Aureus choking on his
tears. "It's alright, I'll get you a coffee, sit on the couch," she said
and walked off to get coffee. "Thank you, Stella, you are a good
friend," he called in the kitchen as he sat on the couch. She returned
with two coffees she put one on the coffee table in front of Aureus, and the
other she held and sat on a chair nearby. "Is Rogue Star alright?"
asked Stella. "She's in love with a Ghost," said Aureus. "Oh no," said
Stella being sympathetic she already knew it, "Are you alright?" "No I
don't know how I will take it in my fragile state," said Aureus.
"Fragile?" said Stella worried. "I am having blackouts, and I am waking
from them in strange places. I seem to be travelling and doing things
when I am in black-outs," admitted Aureus who was beside himself. "I
don't know what I do during them I fear for Rogue's safety." "That is
bad, you do know I'm a doctor of archaeology, not medicine," she
said.

"Yes, I needed to talk to a friend," said Aureus. "Yes, you did right
Aureus," said Stella. "This can't get out I'll be deposed," said Au-reus.

"Yes, I won't tell anyone," she said. "I feel as if I am  living two
lives." said Aureus, "I didn't want to go to the masked ball as the
Ghost I woke up from a blackout walking into the room you were in

dressed like that. It wasn't the only time I found myself dressed as him

I feel like I'm possessed." Then the penny dropped to Stella. He was

not jealous or sad she liked someone else he feared the Ghost, He feared

he may hurt Rogue Star when he was in a black-out. She didn't know what

to do or say. "I was surprised no one recognised the ghost at the party

when I realised who he was," said Aureus. "It's the way you stand and

walk and your eyes. We know you, he looks and moves differently," she

said, "I think we should tell my dad he might know what to do." "Yes he

can help," said Aureus. "Dad we need your help," called Stella. Out of

thin air appeared Jasper. "What's wrong?" asked Jasper seeing His crying

friend. "We know who the Ghost is?" said Stella. "What?" Jasper said

looking from Stella to Aureus. "Why do you two need help? I thought

you'd be happy," said Jasper. "I think I'm possessed," said Aureus.

"Possessed?" said Jasper. "Yes, what should we do?" asked Stella. "There

is only one person who can help us, Rogue," Jasper said thinking Aureus

knew who she was. "Rogue?" said Aureus puzzle, "why didn't you tell me who you were, Stella?" "I didn't think it would help," said Stella, "who

can help?" "Your predecessor the last emperor of the solar system, Blake Alexander, he was the last king of the grim reapers too," said Jasper. "He's in hiding, do you know where he is?" said Stella. Jasper grimaced then said, "He won't be happy." "Why?" asked Aureus. "Gramps we

need your help," said Jasper. Out of thin air appeared the most unexpected person. "You," said Aureus in disbelief a seeing the person

who arrived. "What do you want boy," grumbled the annoyed former

emperor. "Why are you hiding?" said Stella. "Obvious! They'll depose me

again," moaned Sapphirus shaking his head. "Yes," agreed Aureus. Blake

was deposed from his job as a dead man him being a grim reaper. "What do

you want," Blake moaned. "You know the Ghost?" said Jasper. "Who

doesn't?" said Blake. "He's possessing Aureus," said Jasper. Blake looked at Aureus. "No he's not," said Blake. "He is, I black out and keep appearing dressed as him," said Aureus. "Very possible," said Blake. "Then you believe me?" said Aureus. "You aren't possessed," said

Blake. "What?" said Aureus. "Then what is happening if he's not possessed?" Jasper asked. "He is not possessed he is him," Blake said. "I am the Ghost?" said Aureus his eyes widening. "Yes," said Blake, "have you heard of reincarnation?" "Of course, the spirit lives many lives, your ex-wife, or is she your wife now? She was reincarnated," said Aureus. "Yes," said Blake. "How can he be back?" asked Aureus.

"He awoke from his sleep," said Blake, "do any of you know anything that could have awoken him?" "Wait a minute," Stella said ran off and searched her bedroom for something. She returned with something in a box. "What is it?" Jasper asked. She opened the box it was the Ghost's gun. "When I first touched I felt something funny and I saw him!" said Stella. Blake smiled. "That's it," said Blake, "It contains part of his soul It woke him up." "Oh it's Hawk- trucks or something," said Aureus. "That's Harry Potter this is real life," said Blake, "where did you find it?" "26 years ago in Essex England, I excavated it," said Stella. "You aren't old enough to have done that," said her father. "Did you get help going there," asked Blake figuring out what happened. "Yes, I heard a voice call me to go into a portal to get the lost gun of the Ghost. I found a man there he said he was my-" said Stella who was interrupted by Blake who said, "Tempus, he did this he was using your interest in the Ghost to wake him up." "Should I ignore him?" asked Stella. "No, he helps us when he's not watching or using us," Blake said. "Can we put the Ghost to sleep?" asked Aureus. "Not without you reverting to the Masked Chicken and your empire falling. I believe that was why Tempus wanted to

wake up the Ghost he is helping you." "How making me Jekyll and Hyde"

asked Aureus. "I believe it was 26 years ago was when you lost the Masked Chicken the Ghost is the soul of the Rose," said Blake. The Rose had

indeed woken up when the gun was touched it put the Chicken to sleep

never to return. They had to live with the Ghost. Stella and Aureus did

marry and lived together happily ever after.

# CHAPTER SEVEN

# The Clown Show

"Hello, Gramps, who's the clown?" Prince Jasper asked his grandfather

Sapphirus, the emperor of the Universe of a man dressed as a masked

Harlequin.

"The Ghost," said Sapphirus. The Ghost was a man possessed by the ghost of a highwayman called the Ghost.

Prince Jasper's daughter brightened up, she was in love with the Ghost.

"I should have known he's so handsome," said Stella Prince Jasper's daughter admiring the Ghost.

"Hello Stella, nice outfit," said the Ghost, not so pleased to see her she was just a friend to him, she was dressed as a Pierrot clown.

"I'm Pierrot," said Stella.

"Good for you," said the Ghost.

Stella felt like he wasn't noticing her, she felt like a really heartbro-
ken

sad clown, he didn't like her like she wanted, so she left them.

She went to the costume room, which was full of costumes for the
guests

of the ball run by Aureus, the emperor of the local star system

for Sapphirus.

She chose a costume called Columbine, a cute peasant dress with a
mask, she put it on and returned to see the Ghost.

"Hello young lady who are you?" asked the impressed Ghost noticing how the dress clung well to her well-formed figure.

Sapphirus and Prince Jasper looked at each other, knowing who she
was and why she was dressed like that.

"Hello Rogue," said the Ghost, he knew her not as Stella but as her
alter ego, a superhero.

Rogue looked the Ghost over, she liked what she saw, it was obvious
and

embarrassing to see for her father and great-grandfather "Hello Ghost,"

said Rogue. The Ghost was looking at her too.

"Get a room you two," said Sapphirus disgusted. Her father glared at him.

"... Or dance," added Sapphirus noticing his grandson glaring at him for

suggesting his daughter should get a room with a man, she may have been an adult, but he was still her father.

"Oh?" said the embarrassed Rogue, remembering she wasn't alone with the Ghost.

"Ah? Rogue, do you want to dance," asked the nervous Ghost.

"Say yes," said Sapphirus Rogue was so nervous she couldn't speak.

"Yes," said Rogue.

The Ghost leads the nervous Rogue off to dance.

They danced for a while, enjoying each other's company.

Until the emperor saw what Rogue Star hadn't yet.

The possessed man was becoming unpossessed he was turning into another man.

"Excuse me, I need to talk to the Ghost," Sapphirus said to Prince Jasper, leaving him.

"Ok," said Prince Jasper.

Sapphirus walked up to the love birds.

"Hi Sapphirus," said Rogue.

"I have to cut in," said Sapphirus.

"I don't want to dance with you," Rogue said, frowning.

"Good, I don't want to dance with you either," said Sapphirus cutting in and dancing off with the puzzled Ghost, leaving the room.

An invisible unheard voice laughed its head off, seeing it.

Rogue looked puzzled and annoyed seeing her great-grandfather stealing
her dance partner, she walked back to her snickering father who saw it
too.

"What was that about?" asked Rogue.

"Gramps wanted to talk to him," said her father.

Rogue thought it was just a bad dad joke.

Meanwhile, in the costume room.

"Blake, why did you have to do that, I was dancing with Rogue Star,"
said the now completely changed Ghost to Sapphirus using his secret birth
name Blake.

"I noticed," Blake the former local star system's emperor said seriously to the
new one, "You were lucky she didn't notice it, Aureus."

"I wish she did," said Aureus.

"She doesn't love you, you'll break her heart," said Blake.

"Shame," said Aureus sadly.

"Put this on," said Blake, throwing a male Pierrot outfit at him.

"Why this?" said Aureus.

"It's the only thing in your size," said Blake.

"Oh," said Aureus, going into a changing room.

"I'll do the makeup for you," said Blake.

Not long later, Sapphirus returned with Aureus.

"Where did he go?" asked Rogue.

"Hello, Rogue," said Aureus, really happy to see her.

"Nice makeup, did you do it yourself, Aureus?" asked Rogue offhandedly.

"No Sapphirus did it for me," said Aureus, "that is a lovely dress, Rogue."

"Meh!" said Rogue, starting to walk off, fed up with the attention paid

to her by her friend and stalker as Rogue, Aureus, who she didn't love.

Aureus walked up to her and kissed her hand as she left.

"Till we meet again," said Aureus.

"Bye Aureus, nice party," she said and left.

"You'll see her again, Aureus," said Blake, thinking he'd be sad she left.

"She spoke to me," said Aureus happy.

Blake smiled.

Not long after, Stella returned in her Pierrot outfit.

"Hi Stella," said her father, seeing her

"Hi Stella, you won't believe who was here?" Aureus said.

"The Ghost?" she asked.

Aureus looked confused, was she talking about him.

"I met him before, he is so charming and handsome," said Stella excitedly.

Aureus looked awkward.

"No, not him," said Aureus, "Rogue Star was here she is so pretty and lovely, I kissed her hand."

Stella felt sick.

"Bye Aureus, Gramps, Dad," said Stella, who couldn't stand her super fan.

"Where are you going?" Aureus asked.

"I'm looking for the Ghost, he's here somewhere," said Stella.

"I'll do the same good idea, I'll go look for Rogue Star," said Aureus.

"Ok," said Stella.

"Mind if I tag along, we can look together for them," said Aureus.

"Alright," said Stella sadly, and they left.

"I think his chances of finding her are better," said Prince Jasper to his Granddad Blake, who he bade goodbye to also and wandered off.

Blake knew they were looking for each other, they found each other.

Blake laughed when he was alone.

The owner of the unseen, unheard laughter walked up to Blake, it was a grim reaper.

"Hello son," Blake said to his son the reaper, Prince Jasper's father the Necromancer he saw and heard him.

"What's so funny?" The Necromancer asked.

"Haven't you got someone to kill Necromancer?" Blake said and walked off in a huff.

The frustrated reaper grunted and stormed off.

# CHAPTER EIGHT

# Shadows in the Moonlight

## THE ORIGINAL STORY

I t was a cool and crisp night in the Epping Forest, the stagecoach moved amongst the shadows of a full silver moon. which gave the forest a magical glow, thought Mary Gregory a passenger of the coach. Her brother the Magistrate, Sir Thomas Gregory, thought it felt less magical but more eerie and dangerous. he saw highwaymen and footpads in every shadow. the driver was also nervous as highwaymen were known to work these woods.

Suddenly a man with gleaming guns on a white horse rode out of the shadows into the moonlight. he was handsome and well-dressed.

The nervous driver sped up the coach.

The horseman followed at a faster pace. "Stop or I'll shoot!" he shouted.

Firing his pistol he winged the driver who knew the next shot might kill him. So he slowed and stopped the coach.

The rider pulled up to them and dismounted.

"Stand and deliver, your money or your life!" shouted the highwayman

Mary and her brother climbed out of the coach.

"Ah, good evening my lady and Sir Thomas Gregory. It is a lovely evening is it not?" said the Highwayman as he kissed Mary's hand.

"Oh yes, it is!" responded Mary enchanted by the moonlight and his gallantry.

"No, it is not, I would rather have missed this meeting, Faulkner!" said the Magistrate recognising him from wanted posters.

"Faulkner? Not Gentleman John Faulkner?" asked Mary.

"Guilty," said the highwayman smiling behind his mask.

"Your goods please Sir Thomas," added Faulkner pointing a gun at the Magistrate. Mary offered up her jewellery.

"No keep your things, my lady," said Faulkner giving her jewellery back.

Her brother reluctantly handed him his purse of money.

The highwayman next turned to the driver. Whose arm was bleeding badly and holding out his hand for more booty John said. "Now you sir, you should get that arm looked at it looks quite bad!" the driver handed over his valuables.

The Highwayman sent them on their way. Sir Thomas driving, with the driver inside the coach being tended to by Mary.

Two nights later with the weather warmer, a new highwayman was on the road for the first time.

It seemed to be a youth in a black outfit who was enjoying the thrill of riding through the night.  It was the first outing of this new highwayman.

The highwayman who nearly held up a coach, but somebody beat this would be highwayman to it. So turning the horse and heading home was all that could be done.

The next morning the Gregory home had a visitor.

Mary was very excited to meet this famous man she had never met before.

He was a friend of her brother's a famous popular actor who was playing a highwayman on stage in London.

He was a tall handsome man and from the moment Mary saw him she knew she could easily love this man, his name was Sir Justin Beaufort.

"Hello my lady," said the Actor, "I hear that you met a real highwayman the other day I wish I had been with you. They are so thrilling and romantic!"

"Yes they are," agreed Mary.

"No, they are dangerous mercenaries! The driver of the coach died from the wound he got from the highwayman or did you forget that?" asked Sir Thomas.

Sir Justin looked chastened and nervous.

"Did he have a family?" asked Sir Justin.

"More than likely and they'll hang Faulkner now he's killed someone," said Sir Thomas.

"He won't hang! It was an accident," said Mary.

"He shot the man he should have realised there was a chance the man would die!" said Sir Thomas.

"If they get him they will hang him, I'm sure of that!," said Sir Justin sadly.


Later Mary was riding in a coach with Sir Justin and she heard.

"Stand and deliver your money or your life," The voice yelled.

When the coach stopped she leapt out of the coach to see the driver being murdered with a single shot to the heart. For no other reason than that he didn't stop quickly enough.

She was now nervous. This was the feared killer highwayman Terrence the Terror of Essex.

"Hand over your loot! Either give it to me now or I will take it from your body!" Terrence the Terror said to her.

She did so quickly.

Out of the coach stepped an angry Sir Justin.

"That's enough Terry.  Give it all back !" said Sir Justin.

This startled the Terror who was confused. Justin walked over disarmed him and pointed the Terror's own gun at him.

"I said give it back, Terry!" said Sir Justin.

"Don't call him Terry people say he doesn't like that! This isn't the theatre he'll kill you!" said Mary nervously.

"He'll have to wait in line!" said Sir Justin. with a smile.

"Sir Justin you are annoying me. Nobody robs me not even my friends you will pay for this stand down and I will forget it," said Terrence, the Terror.

"Stand and deliver Terry," said Sir Justin.

"He is drunk ignore him, Mister Terror!" said Mary.

"He's stone-cold sober and stubborn!" said the highwayman.

Terrence the Terror handed back the loot but he was fuming.

Sir Justin shot in the air to disarm the gun.

"Here you are, my friend, have your property and let us go on our way." Sir Justin said.

"You are not my friend!" said Terrence the Terror stomping over to his horse.

"You know something I think I have lost a friend!" said Sir Justin sadly as he drove the coach off.

"You are insane!" shouted back Mary from inside the coach.

Later in the day at the Gregory home.

"Tom your friend is a nut!" Mary said when they arrived with the body of the driver.

"What did he do murder the driver so he could drive the coach?" asked Sir Thomas.

Sir Justin laughed.

"No that was Terrence the Terror!" said Sir Justin.

"Oh did he kill the driver so you could drive it?" said Sir Thomas

"Are you insane!" asked Sir Justin.

"No," said Sir Thomas

"Terrence the Terror held us up, he shot the driver, then I held up the Terror!" said Sir Justin.

"You did what? " asked Sir Thomas.

"I bailed up the Terror and took your sister's stuff back as she was under my care!" said Sir Justin.

"Thank you did you take him in?" asked Sir Thomas.

"No! I let him go!" said Sir Justin.

"Why did you do that!" asked Sir Thomas.

"Someone had to drive the coach, and I could not be sure of Mary's safety if I kept him," replied Sir Justin.

"You know that he'll now try to kill you!" said Sir Thomas.

"If he does he does!  I could never live with myself if he robbed someone under my care!"  replied Sir Justin.


That night the youthful highwayman rode again.

This time he stopped a coach and started to rob people when three highwaymen arrived on the scene.

"New to this are you lad!" said one of them.

The youth panicked and fell off the horse banging his head hard and was knocked out by the fall.

"Terry I think you killed him!" said one of the others he was the black-clad highwayman named the Ghost for his sudden appearances and disappearances

"Ghost the boy's knocked out! Not dead," said Gentleman John who was riding with them.

"Terry just scared him," said John.

"We can't leave him here what will we do!" said the Highwayman the Ghost,  a Robin Hood-type highwayman.

They completed the robbery.

John picked the body up and hung it over his horse.

The Ghost took the horse of the young highwayman and they rode off to Gentleman John's house.

"I'll look after him till he comes round!" offered John.

The odd band of highwaymen sat drinking and chatting for a few hours and then the Terror and the ghost left. When they had gone John made a strange discovery the boy had long hair in a bun and his hat had been pinned to it. He found this out when he tried to remove the hat so he could put the lad to rest on his bed.

He put her on the bed and sat looking at a script for a new play.

He then sat drinking for a while.

Later when the highwaywoman woke up it was like a play with a ham actor.

"Where am I?" she muttered.

Putting down the script he walked over to her.

"How are you feeling Miss?" asked John.

"Miss?'" said the highwaywoman not sure how he knew what she was or where she was.

She felt for her mask it was there.

"I saw your hair! If we knew you were a woman my friends would have stayed," said John.

"Why?" she asked.

"For your honour," said John, "Whoever said there is no honour among thieves?"

"Oh yes!" said the highwaywoman.

"Nothing happened but I'll marry you to keep your honour," said John.

The highwaywoman stood up still a bit wonky. She thought she was dreaming he was a man of honour and she loved him so she was happy.

She started to take off her mask and he stopped her.

"No don't," said John. "we aren't safe, Seeing each other's faces may cause us problems!"

"All right then!" She said and stopped trying to unmask.

In the early morning, she said goodbye and left for home.

A few hours later, Mary was sitting in the forest near her home enjoying the new autumn day.

Sir Justin saw her on the way to visit her brother.

He got off his horse and tied it to a branch of a small tree and walked over to her.

"What are you doing my lady?" asked Sir Justin thinking she looked very pretty sitting amongst the autumn leaves. She blushed.

"It is ethereal here today!" said  Mary looking at Sir Justin who looked more handsome than ever.

"It is a glorious day!" said Sir Justin not lying,

"Are you alright?"

"Yes, come sit beside me," said Mary.

"Why?" asked Sir Justin.

"The view is best from here," said Mary.

"As long as no one's around!" said Sir Justin.

With a smile, she said, "No one is here!"

Sir Justin sat beside her.

"What are we looking at?" asked Sir Justin.

"Everything the wind is singing in the trees blowing leaves through the air as they fall to the ground. The birds are singing and the forest floor is covered in crisp leaves thick as snow," said Mary.

Forgetting propriety and everything. He lay on his back in the leaves.

"I have never seen anything so beautiful! I could forget everything and live here in this moment forever," then looking up at the sky. He said, "This looks better!"

Mary lay back too she watched the leaves fall from the trees blowing in the wind.  A leaf fell down floating onto her heart she put her hand on it.

A voice interrupted the scene.

"There you are, Mary, have you been with him all night?  Everyone has been looking for you!" accused Sir Thomas.

"No!" Sir Justin said standing. "I just found her here, I was on my way to see you."

Mary trying to stand up fell over her long skirt.

"I was not with him!" said Mary.

Sir Justin thought he could see a forced Marriage wedding being set up.

"I can't marry her!" said Sir Justin.

"Why?" asked Sir Thomas.

"I can't say!" said Sir Justin.

"No excuses means that you must marry her for your honour and hers," said Sir Thomas.

"Don't use my honour against me!" said Sir Justin.

"You must Marry her as you are driven by your honour," Sir Thomas said.

Sir Justin shook his head jumped on his horse and rode away.


Over the following weeks, the Highwayman and  Highwaywoman became inseparable and took to the road most nights. They planned to run away and marry after one last job but it all went wrong.  there was an unexpected ambush.

They were on their horses and when they demanded the passengers disembark the coach. they didn't notice the gun pointing from the coach until it was too late. but when they did they rode away it was Sir Thomas who shot one of them.

John could have escaped. but he jumped off his running horse which continued on its way. He ran back to his fiancée the Highwaywoman.

"You shot her!" said John accusingly

Kneeling down cradling her and looking into her face.

"Why didn't you escape?" asked the dying Highwaywoman.

"I don't want to live without you!" said John.

"I have the two of them! I shall unmask them," said Sir Thomas. unmasking John his eyes widened and looked horrified.

"Hi!" said Sir Justin.

"You are engaged to my sister! Who is this Harlot?" asked Sir Thomas ripping off her mask. Looking devastated.

"Mary! No!" cried Sir Thomas.

"Mary my other fiancée?" said John.

"My love!" said Mary and died.

John kissed her for the first and last time.



A few weeks later John joined her in death.

As John was standing on the gallows at Tyburn.

Sir Thomas watched the noose go round John's neck  Sir Thomas was sad he knew he'd miss John and Justin.  The executioner reached for and pulled the lever for the trap door. Then the Magistrate closed his eyes. He saw Mary and John lying in the leaves in the forest and he heard John saying "I have never seen anything so beautiful! I could forget everything and live in this moment forever"

The End

# CHAPTER NINE

# In the Moonlight: a highwayman song

[Spoken]
"Stand and deliver, your money or your life!"
[Chorus]
In the moonlight,
I ride the dark roads of night,
as the leaves float by,

[Verse]
Stand and deliver, I cry,
By the moonlight,
I ride,
[Chorus]
In the moonlight,
I ride the dark roads of night,

as the leaves float by,
[Coda]
I will ride til I die
on these night roads,
I'll ride with the wind and the moonlight to the night's end,
In the daylight

# CHAPTER TEN

# Midnight Requiem Song

Darkness conceals its beauty within an aura of fear,

Night to me is something dear,

In the coolness of the night, I ride,

The wary do cautiously hide,

In fear of me and my cast,

I alone see the night's beauty to its hour's last,

Like a thief in the night,

When I'm seen, I disappear like a ghost out of sight

# CHAPTER ELEVEN

# The Ghost of Your Gaze or The Ghost's Serenade a song

[Spoken]
"What are you doing?"
"Why are you dressed
as the Ghost?"

[Chorus]
I'm a ghost,
I'm not ghosting you.
I am here, although you don't see me,
I am here, but you can't hear me,
All you see is another man,

With my face, and form,

[Verse 1]
You can see me through his facade,
I am the one who truly loves you,
but you see me as only a friend,
to you, I am merely a shade of myself.

[Chorus]
I'm a ghost,
I'm not ghosting you.
I am here, although you don't see me,
I am here, but you can't hear me,
All you see is another man,
With my face, and form,

[Chorus]
I'm a ghost,
I'm not ghosting you.
I am here, although you don't see me,
I am here, but you can't hear me,
All you see is another man,
With my face, and form,

[Verse 2]
Why can't you see me beyond the echos of the past,
Why are you blind to my love?
Will you ever see me?
The true me

[Chorus]

I'm a ghost,

I'm not ghosting you.

I am here, although you don't see me,

I am here, but you can't hear me,

All you see is another man,

With my face, and form,

[Coda]

I'm a ghost,

I'm not ghosting you.

I am here, although you don't see me,

I am here, but you can't hear me,

All you see is another man,

With my face, and form,

[Spoken]

"But you are no Ghost he is charming and amazing, you are just...
You."

"Well, I could be him, he is very mysterious,"

# CHAPTER TWELVE

# Dick Turpin & the King of the Road a Song

Upon the road, Tom, the King of the road, met Turpin,
Dick thought Tom King was a fat pigeon,
they rode together on their way,
they robbed people with their guns under the code of the men of the highway,

"Your money or your life?" they did call,
it was nothing or all,
Tom made Turpin a highwayman legend,
it was rumoured Turpin brought King to his end,
Tom was shot in the shoulder,
he was taken to the Doctor,
he could not be saved,
Turpin, goodbye to the road he waved,

a butcher he became,
he was caught under a charge of a poaching claim,
he wrote a letter for help from one of his in-laws,
the only problem was the letter his death did cause,
an old teacher of Turpin's read through his fraud,
they knew his handwriting he told the truth and no one could save
him, not even the good Lord.


He was revealed and caught,
the gallows called according to the court.
death came swiftly,
the legend grew greater hereby quickly.

# CHAPTER THIRTEEN

# Death Called To Me

## A SONG

I wander lost and alone in a world I do not know,

Nobody sees or hears my cries,

I am dead, I know not,

where I am or where I will go,

I followed Death's call, and he left me alone and scared,

I don't know if he will come back for me,

I know not what am,

I know not where I go to,

I know not where this will end,

or if this solitary sentence will ever end,


I wander lost and alone in a world I do not know,

Nobody sees or hears my cries,

I am dead, I know not,

where I am or where I will go,

I followed Death's call, and he left me alone and scared,

I don't know if he will come back for me,

I know not what am,

I know not where I go to,

I know not where this will end,

or if this solitary sentence will ever end.

# About the author

Rachel is a lover of gothic
   poetry and the stories of Emily Dickinson, Poe, and other poets
and
   writers. She writes in a gothic sometimes romantic, and somewhat
   eclectic style

Is a classic, prolific writer.

Contact Rachel via her website

Where she writes
https://allpoetry.com/The_Poette

Good Reads Page
https://www.goodreads.com/author/show/17771936.Rachel_La
wson

Website

http://www.rachellawsonpoet.yolasite.com/


YouTube songs are sung here

https://www.youtube.com/@BlakeAlexander-kq8qq


Spotify Artist Profile

https://open.spotify.com/artist/1G9bsRFWnpq2RgNcrJ7Jmw?s
i=SvwykHkxQtGarCJM6Ijefw


Rachel Lawson, YouTube Topic

https://www.youtube.com/channel/UC2L3-DWz4IupjemyvNvf
rwA


Song Death Called to Me on YouTube

https://youtu.be/y9UcyVqiXjs

# Blurb

## BEST LINES FROM STORY THE KING'S MAN

"What are you doing my lady?" asked Sir Justin thinking she looked very pretty sitting amongst the autumn leaves. She blushed.

"It is ethereal here today!" said Mary looking at Sir Justin who looked more handsome than ever.

"It is a glorious day!" said Sir Justin not lying,

"Are you alright?"

"Yes, come sit beside me," said Mary.

"Why?" asked Sir Justin.

"The view is best from here," said Mary.

"As long as no one's around!" said Sir Justin.

With a smile, she said, "No one is here!"

Sir Justin sat beside her.

"What are we looking at?" asked Sir Justin.

"Everything the wind is singing in the trees blowing leaves through the air as they fall to the ground. The birds are singing and the forest floor is covered in crisp leaves thick as snow," said Mary.

Forgetting propriety and everything. He lay on his back in the leaves.

"I have never seen anything so beautiful, I could forget everything and live here in this moment forever." then looking up at the sky He said, "This looks better!"